MAKING the SHADOW-PUPPET STAGE

1. What you'll need:

One Old Sheet

2 Thumb Tacks

A Lamp

2. Tack the sheet to hang in front of an open doorway.

3. Position the lamp to project on the upper-half of the sheet.

4. Sitting on the floor, between the lamp and the sheet, hold the puppet above your head, in front of the light.

This will project a shadow on the sheet.

5. Invite an audience to sit on the other side of the hanging sheet – where they can watch your shadow-puppet dance and play!

Peppy's Shadow

written by **Marcia Trimble**

illustrated by **Will Pellegrini**

Published by Images Press

Publisher's Cataloging-in-Publication
(Provided by Quality Books, Inc.)

Trimble, Marcia.
     Peppy's shadow / written by Marcia Trimble ; illustrated by Will Pellegrini -- 1st ed.
     p. cm.
     SUMMARY: Peppy the puppy discovers that chasing, gnawing, chewing, barking and pulling can turn into positive talents and proudly walks in her own shadow. Includes puppet patterns and directions for making a shadow puppet stage.
     Audience: Ages 4-8.
     LCCN: 2002107055
     ISBN: 1-891577-70-0 (HC)
     ISBN: 1-891577-71-9 (PB)

1. Dogs--Juvenile fiction. 2. Shadow puppets--Juvenile Fiction.
[1. dogs--Fiction. 2. Shadow puppets--Fiction.]   I. Pellegrini, Will.
II. Title.

PZ7.T335Pe 2003   [E]
                         QBI02-701643

10 9 8 7 6 5 4 3 2 1

Text set in Tweed and Becka Script.
Book design by MontiGraphics.
Manufactured in China
by South China Printing Co. Ltd.
on Lumi Matte Art paper;
chlorine free.

To Peppy.
- M. T.

To my friends, Colin and Pito.
- W. P.

...into a magical world of **light** and **shadows.**

Peppy played backstage while Pepito,
the shadow puppet, tap danced...

...and did tricks on his trapeze.

"If only I had a partner who would be my friend" thought Pepito...

as visions of a shadow partner danced in his head.

...dumped her dogfood...

...chewed on slippers and shoes...

The Diva walked by
and sang a tune
Peppy had heard before.

"Peppy, sit."

"Good girl," sang the Diva.

"Peppy, down," said the stagehand.
Peppy slipped down beside her dogfood dish.
"Good dog," said the stagehand.

Peppy licked the costume designer
but never the shoes.
"Good Peppy," said the costume designer.

Peppy slept near the birdcage
but she ignored the bird.
The sound designer patted Peppy's head.

Peppy snuggled in the chair
but she didn't sniff
the stuffing.
The set designer
stroked her back.

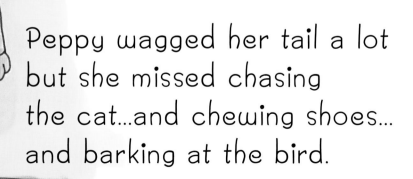

Peppy wagged her tail a lot
but she missed chasing
the cat...and chewing shoes...
and barking at the bird.

One day Peppy noticed patterns of light on the floor. She stared at the shadows jiggling on the rug.

She jumped at the shadow moving on the wall.

PEPPY

Puppet Making
The numbers and letters tell you where the arms and legs go.

PEPITO

3

2   1

4   3

1

4

2

2

She chased
the shadow
of her tail.

She spun
'round
and
'round...

until...

Peppy CHASED and GNAWED at the
the shadow...   leg of the shadow...

The director ran over to Peppy. "Good Peppy," he said!
"You saved Pepito. You saved the show."
"Good girl," said the puppetmaster.

"You're an angel, Peppylita," said Lupe.

Pepito danced around Peppy...
and patted her nose.

Pepito smiled his cardboard boy smile.
He had found a partner...and a friend.

Between shows,

Lupe took Peppy outside for walks.

With an air of satisfaction...

STAGE
DOOR
←

Peppy walked in her own shadow!

MAKE YOUR OWN SHADOW-PUPPET

1. What you'll need:

 Scotch Tape

6 Brass Brads

4 Popsicle Sticks

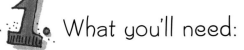

2. Punch out the pieces of the shadow-puppets. Make sure to punch out the eyes and Pepito's mouth, as well.

3. Using the brass brads, attach the two arms and two legs to Pepito's body.

4. Using brads, attach the two sets of legs to Peppy's body.

5. Using the scotch tape, attach the popsicle sticks to the back-sides of Pepito's feet and Peppy's feet.

Now that you've made two shadow-puppets, learn how to make a shadow-puppet stage...